# MATT SADLER

## By Ed Dolphin

*To Joel
Best wishes
Ed Dolphin*

Lawn Primary School

Published in 2009 by New Generation Publishing

Copyright ©Text Ed Dolphin

First Edition

The author asserts the moral right under the Copyright, Designs and Patents Act 1988 to be identified as the author of this work.

All rights reserved. No part of this publication may be reproduced, stored in a retrieval system, or transmitted in any form or by any means without the prior written consent of the author, nor be otherwise circulated in any form of binding or cover other than that in which it is published and without a similar condition being imposed on the subsequent purchaser.

# Matt Sadler

| | |
|---|---|
| The Granscher | 1 |
| Gerble | 15 |
| Disappointment | 27 |
| The Trap | 34 |
| Lord Stermian | 44 |
| Homeward | 56 |
| Return | 64 |
| Closure | 70 |
| Rest | 80 |

## Chapter 1 – THE GRANSCHER!

Matthew Sadler whistled happily as he walked out of the forest, his red leather bag was slung over one shoulder and his fine leather cloak over the other.

He had been travelling towards the mountains but now he found himself on the edge of the market square of a village. It looked like his own village, whitewashed houses of different sizes with thatched roofs, but something made him stop whistling. It was like a ghost town, there was no one to be seen, no people, no animals in the fields, not even a cat sat on a doorstep. There must have been people in the little stone houses because of the smoke curling lazily from some of the chimneys and Matthew could definitely smell food cooking.

Something caught his eye. The first of the mountains rose beyond the village, and high up there was something sparkling in the early morning sunshine. 'Treasure,' Matthew thought to himself and he smiled.

Suddenly he heard a shout.

"Get inside you fool! The Granscher will get you!" A man was calling and waving from the doorway of the inn. He looked so frantic that Matthew ran over to him. The man reached out, grabbed Matthew's arm and dragged him inside. Just then, there was a great swooping noise but also a musical jingling. A huge shadow swept across the sunlit market place but the gloom was sprinkled with multicoloured flashes.

"That was lucky," sighed the man who had pulled Matthew inside to safety.

"What on earth was it?" Matthew asked with a slightly shaken voice.

The man looked nervously over his shoulder and then whispered the word 'Granscher'.

"What's a Granscher?"

"It's a fearsome beast, a dragon with huge leathery wings, terrifying claws, teeth like jagged knives."

"Wow, that sounds exciting," Matthew let out a long whistle.

"Exciting? It's blinking dangerous!" The man gave Matthew a funny look. "The Granscher has made our lives a misery. It eats our animals, it even eats people if it gets the chance."

"Noooh," Matthew gasped.

"The Granscher has amazing eyesight," the man hooded his eyes with his chubby right hand for effect. "It sits high in the mountains watching the village square. If it sees a person or an animal, it will swoop down and snatch them up in its vicious claws!" The man's hand swept down from his brow and grasped thin air in an upturned fist. "That's why the square was so quiet when you came into the village, all the people are hiding indoors and all the animals: cats, dogs, sheep, goats, all the animals are locked away." The man shook his head.

"That's terrible," said Matthew. "But how do you survive? How do you live?"

"We've become nocturnal, we live at night," the man said wearily. "We go to work at night, we have our market at night, even our sheep and goats are taken out to graze at night. We sleep during the day, I was just on my way to bed when I heard you whistling."

"Is it safe at night then?"

"Oh yes, the Granscher cannot fly in the dark. It can sit in its cave on the mountain and spot a cat down here on the square if the sun is shining, but in the dark it is completely blind."

"Why doesn't someone go and kill the Granscher at night then?"

"Some people tried… when the Granscher first appeared. My own father was one…" The man looked down at his feet and sighed. "The scales defeated them all."

"The scales?"

"Yes, the Granscher's body is covered in scales. They look beautiful, they shimmer with rainbow colours like the feathers on a peacock's tail, but they're actually the Granscher's best weapons. They've got jagged edges like saw blades, and they're so hard no sword, spear or arrow could pierce them. It's the scales that make it jingle as it flies."

"But it sounded so lovely," Matthew said.

"Lovely yes, but deadly. Anyway," the man changed the subject. "Tell us about yourself, we don't often see strangers in these parts, well not for long, if you know what I mean."

"I'm Matthew, Matthew Sadler, good morning." Matthew held out a hand and the man shook it.

"Bert, Bert Brewer, I'm the innkeeper here. So Matthew, what brings you to our village?"

"I'm travelling the world, seeking my fortune."

"Your fortune would be secure if you could kill the Granscher," Bert let out a deep laugh. "The whole village would reward you, but that's just a dream, no-one can defeat that awful monster." The innkeeper sighed and then shrugged. "In any case, looking at your fine leather cloak and red leather bag, you can't be that poor to start with."

"I've my dad to thank for that. As his name suggests, he's a saddler, the finest worker of leather in our county."

"From the look of his work, I'd say you're right there."

"Yes, he and mother didn't really want me to travel but, when I insisted that I needed to go, he said that he'd make the cloak to protect me and the bag to hold my things."

"So, where is your county?"

"West Fennyland, it's a long journey, I'm not sure how far, but I've been travelling for several weeks now."

"Right young sir, now that you are here and safe, can I offer you something to eat?"

"Yes, thank you," Matthew replied gratefully.

Matthew sat eating the meal, a delicious plate of ham and eggs, but he was thinking hard while he chewed. When he had mopped the last dribble of yolk with a piece of freshly baked bread, he pushed the plate back and looked out of the window.

"As I said, it is time for my bed." Bert stretched and yawned.

"But I'm not tired, I camped in the forest last night and slept, wrapped in my lovely cloak, as soundly as the logs that were set beside my fire. I will sit here and amuse myself if that's all right with you."

"Please yourself, but you'll be up all tonight, this place gets really busy once the sun's gone down."

"I suppose so," Matthew agreed. "I'll take a nap later." He rose and went to the window.

"Just remember, whatever you do, don't go outside," Bert warned.

"Don't worry, I'll not be going out." Matthew looked out of the window and up at the mountain. "Goodnight, or should I say good morning."

"Good day," corrected the innkeeper with a smile. "The guest room is just at the top of the stairs should you want to lie down. Help yourself to food and drink, we can settle up this evening. Remember, whatever you do, don't go outside." His voice had a deathly serious tone. With that, he went off up his stairs to bed.

Matthew spent the morning walking up and down inside the inn. It was frustrating to be inside on such a lovely day and, from time to time, he peered out of the window and up at the nearby mountain. West Fennyland was a very flat land near a wide river, Matthew had never seen even a steep hill before setting off on his travels, let alone a mountain. He was impressed by this mountain although it was, compared to great mountains of other lands, only a small one. The winter's snow had already melted from all but the topmost peak.

Matthew could see a black thing two thirds of the way up the mountain, was it a cave? He wasn't sure, but was that a glint of something shiny moving around near it? His question was soon answered.

A fox had come sniffing around the edge of the village square, hunting for scraps. Matthew watched it as it went from house to house seeking out the dustbins with its sensitive nose. Suddenly the fox froze, something had alarmed it. It looked up and then turned and ran. It ran back across the village square towards the edge of the forest, but it didn't reach the safety of the trees. A huge glittering shape shot across the open space and the fox vanished.

Matthew was stunned, but then he looked back to the mountain. He saw the Granscher, its body sparkling in the sunshine as the dark grey wings carried it back to its lair. The fox hung limp, grasped firmly in the Granscher's talons.

The Granscher didn't look like any dragon that Matthew had seen in his story books. It didn't have a long tail and its neck was not particularly long. Its body was more the shape of a man, and its wings were like those of the bats that fluttered near the river when he fished on a summer evening. But these wings didn't flutter, they were much too big, they beat majestically against the morning air.

The Granscher grew smaller and smaller as it flew up. Finally, it was just a glittering speck that vanished into the black mark that was the mouth of its cave.

"I'm glad the innkeeper heard me whistling," Matthew muttered to himself. The thought of his lucky escape made him feel weary and so he climbed the stairs and settled into the bed. After several nights of sleeping in the forest, the bed was so comfortable that he soon fell asleep, but his dreams were troubled by monsters and devils trying to kill him.

Matthew was woken by the sound of voices. It was dark in the room. He roused himself from the bed, the bedding was all tangled as if he had been fighting all night – or all day. He went downstairs and the inn was busy.

"Hello there, you must be Matthew." A tall man stepped forward and offered Matthew his hand. "Bob, Bob Sawyer, I do all the local woodwork for people." The hand was strong and the skin tougher than the leather of Matthew's bag. Several other villagers welcomed Matthew cheerfully, there wasn't the usual silence that greets a stranger in a closed community. Matthew spent time talking with many of them. They were all good people who wanted to know about his travels, but Matthew was more keen to hear about their lives with the threat of the Granscher. The difficulty became clear close to midnight.

"Well Matthew, it's been good to talk, but I've got to go to work now," Bob Sawyer said. "What about you Bill Shepherd? Isn't it about time you let your flock out of their barn?" One by one, the villagers finished their drink, waved goodbye and went out into the dark. One by one the lights went on in the shops and workshops as they opened, and animals made their way out to the fields led by men carrying lanterns.

"It all looks so pretty," Matthew said to Bert. "We hang lanterns around our village at the mid-winter festival."

"That's all very well, but we'd like the lanterns to be for special occasions, not every day."

"I suppose so," Matthew sympathised.

Later, as the grey light of dawn spread across the village, some villagers returned to the inn after their hard night's work. They didn't stay long and soon began to bid each other good day and, one by one, they went off to their houses, moving quickly with regular glances up at the mountain.

As the inn emptied, Matthew was sat quietly by the fire, deep in thought. Bert had just finished washing all the pots and was about to wish him good day when, suddenly, Matthew jumped to his feet.

"I've had an idea," he announced grandly. "I'm going to get rid of that Granscher for you!"

The innkeeper was worried. Excitedly, Matthew explained what he was going to do.

"You're crazy!" Bert said shaking his head. "You'll get killed. You'd do much better to have some sleep and then go on your way this evening. Your parents will want you to return safely, with or without your fortune."

When he thought about it, Matthew realised that his idea was a bit mad, but he had never really experienced any danger during his very comfortable upbringing, and so he wasn't good at weighing up how perilous things could be. He thought it would all work out in the end because things always had done before.

"Don't do it," Bert held Matthew by the arm, but Matthew picked up his cloak and strode bravely out into the market square.

High in the mountains, the Granscher was sat hunched by its cave entrance. It was angry that it had only eaten a skinny fox in the last few days. As Matthew marched out under the brightening sky, the Granscher couldn't miss him. Its keen eyesight recognised the juicy breakfast that had disappeared so suddenly inside the inn door the previous day. Its vile green tongue licked the horny lips, it spread its monstrous wings and launched itself from the rocky crag. Thoughts of delicious human flesh were in its mind as it flew down.

In the market square, Matthew stood right out in the middle, watching. He saw the glittering speck as the Granscher's body caught the first rays of the rising sun, and he stood still as it grew bigger and bigger, coming closer and closer.

"Come back in you fool!" Bert shouted from his doorway but Matthew just stood looking up.

"It's okay, I know what I'm doing," Matthew shouted. *'At least, I hope I do,'* he muttered to himself.

All round the square there were faces at the windows looking to see what the shouting was about, and people were moaning and shaking their heads. "What do you think you're doing?" Bob Sawyer called. Others called out warnings, but Matthew held up his hand and said that he was all right. He stood his ground as the Granscher closed in. It had reached the roofs of the houses at the end of the street, it seemed to fill the sky as it stretched its terrifying claws, ready to strike.

All of a sudden, Matthew whipped off his cloak, whirled it around his head and threw it up in the air. At the same time, he threw himself flat on the ground.

Whoosh! The Granscher swooped down but its claws missed him. The cloak wrapped itself around the awful face. The Granscher rose into the air giving out a muffled scream, a scream of anger at missing its meal again, but also a scream of confusion because it was blinded by the cloak.

The Granscher spiralled higher and higher, shaking its head, trying to throw off the cloak. It scratched at it with its clawed feet, but the leather caught on the rough edges of the body scales and it was stuck fast.

The Granscher flew round and round. It tried to use its keen sense of smell to follow its own scent and fly back to its cave.

By now, everyone in the village had their heads poked out of windows and doors watching. Some ventured out into the market place and stood staring and pointing as the Granscher zigzagged its way up to the mountain. They wondered what was going to happen.

Then there was a sickening crunch and a scream that could be heard all the way down in the village as the Granscher missed the cave entrance and hit the sheer face of rock. An avalanche of boulders tumbled down the mountain side, a shower of scales glittered and gleamed as they fell through the sunlit air.

The whole village stood or craned their necks out of the windows and doors for a moment with mouths open. Then someone let out an almighty 'Yippee' and everyone began to dance and sing.

"What a wonderful day," Bert shouted. "Let's have a party, the drinks are on me!"

"I've a fresh batch of cakes," the baker said and danced round in a circle. "And some pies."

"We've not had a hog roast for years," the butcher called. "Come on, let's roast a pig."

People dashed into their homes and pulled tables out into the market square. They loaded them with food and drink and the party started.

Everyone was enjoying the sunshine. For some of them, it was the first time they'd been out in the sun in their lives.

Bert the innkeeper stood on a table and called everyone to order. "Good people," he said grandly. "For years we have lived, quite literally, in the shadow of that monster. Today, we celebrate the lifting of a terrible darkness and it is thanks to our brave new friend, I propose a toast to Matthew Sadler."

Everyone cheered, raised mugs and glasses and shouted "To Matthew, Matthew Sadler!"

Matthew felt rather strange, he was embarrassed to be the centre of so much attention, but he rather enjoyed the feeling.

As the party continued, and people became even more merry, they all wanted to talk with Matthew and give him their own, personal thank you. His hand was pumped to soreness and his shoulder began to ache with all the slaps and pats it received. Then Bert climbed, rather shakily, onto the table again.

"Ladeege and gentlemen," he slurred drunkenly. "Thish fine young man," he waved an arm more or less in Matthew's direction. "Thish fine young man issh travelling the world sheeking hish fortune. I do remember promising that, if he rid ush of the Granscher, the whole village would reward him. Well, I thin' you should keep my promish… if you know what I mean. I will start ush off. Matthew, I hereby present you with a token of our appreciation." With that, he pulled a gold coin from his moneybag, waved it in the air, and promptly fell off the table. Everyone laughed and cheered. The tipsy innkeeper clambered to his feet and walked unsteadily to the table where Matthew was sat. He placed the coin on the table with an extravagant wave of the arm. There were several cries of 'Here, here!' and then several other coins appeared. In no time at all, Matthew had a pile of gold coins spread in front of him.

"Speech, speech," several voices chorused.

Matthew stood up with a very red face. "Well, I'm completely flummoxed," he beamed. "All I can say is, er- thank you." He spread his arms and shrugged his shoulders. The villagers were so delighted with what he had achieved, they didn't mind that the young hero was too tongue-tied to make a speech.

As night set in, instead of setting off for work, the villagers rolled and staggered happily to their beds.

The next day, Matthew and some of the braver villagers climbed up to view the remains of the Granscher. There wasn't much to see because it had been buried in the avalanche. There was just a black stain as if the Granscher's blood had soaked the rocks, and lots of the beautiful scales scattered around. Matthew managed to pull his cloak out from under a boulder. Small pieces of bone and a few jagged teeth clattered and rattled back down into the crevices.

"These will make a beautiful necklace for my mother," he said as he collected some of the iridescent scales.

All the children of the village crowded round Matthew when the exploration party came back down.

"Did you see the Granscher's body?" one boy asked.

"Was it gruesome?" another called.

"Just look at this," Matthew said as he pulled one of the scales from his pocket and it sparkled in the sun. All the children gasped. Matthew beamed, he was enjoying himself.

A few days later, Matthew came down the inn stairs with his bag and cloak. "I need to be off, Bert. Your hospitality has been wonderful, but it's time to go home."

"Surely you can stay a few more days," Bert pleaded.

"You and the villagers have been so kind, but I really need to get back, I know my mother will be worried about me."

"Yes, I suppose you're right."

Matthew stepped out into the market square, bustling in the spring sunshine. Everyone waved and called hello.

"Matthew's going home," Bert called out. Everyone begged him to stay, but, after many handshakes and hugs, Matthew waved them farewell and set off. His leather cloak was tattered and torn from its tangle with the Granscher, but it covered his bag that was now bulging and clinking with gold coins, along with a few glittering Granscher scales.

As for the villagers, they put their lives back to normal, working during the day and going to bed at night. Bob Sawyer was especially happy, the Granscher's scales made super tools for cutting and shaping wood. He carved a plaque with a picture of Matthew blinding the Granscher and it was put up in the market place to remind everyone of the story.

## Chapter 2 – GERBLE

"Look everybody, it's Matthew, Matthew Sadler's back." Matthew's mother came running out of her house when she heard the shout.

"Oh my lord, just look at you." She rushed along the road and threw her arms round her son's neck. The red leather bag on Matthew's shoulder clinked loudly. "But what's this?" She patted the bag and it clinked again. "And just look at your lovely cloak, what have you been up to? Are you hurt? Oh, my poor baby, I knew I shouldn't have let you go." She hugged him even more tightly and the tears flowed freely.

"Mother," Matthew chided. "I'm all right, don't fuss."

Matthew peeled his mother from him, put an arm around her shoulder and started walking her back to the house. By now an excited crowd had gathered and, chattering among themselves, they followed.

"I don't know, just look at the state of that cloak."

"I know, shocking isn't it, his father will be furious, he went to a lot of trouble to make that cloak."

"It looks like he's been sleeping rough, who'd of thought Mrs Sadler's precious son would turn out to be a tramp."

All of a sudden, the strap on Matthew's bag gave way. The bag hit the ground with a thump and a clinking sound and gold coins spilled out onto the dusty road. The crowd froze and there was a united gasp. Matthew's mother broke the spell.

"Matthew! What's going on?" Her voice was shocked and slightly worried.

Matthew collected himself very quickly and announced grandly, "I told you I was going to seek my fortune, well, I found it."

All hell broke loose, everyone crowded forward and there was a confused babble of questions and opinions.

"Did he rob a bank? I bet he robbed a bank."

"No, he's too nice a young man to do something like that."

"I knew he'd turn out to be something special…"

"D'you think that's real gold?"

"He was my best friend at school, me and Matthew thought about getting married when he returned from his travels..."

Matthew felt really pleased that the crowd was centred on him. He held up both hands. "Hold on everybody, hold on. If you must know, this is my reward for killing a dragon."

"Liar!" A tall girl with long black hair pushed through the crowd. She looked almost the same age as Matthew, but she had a mean look in her eye. "You couldn't kill a dragon, and anyway, there aren't any dragons, only in children's stories."

Matthew went very red in the face. "Well you're wrong there Sarah Alport. There *are* dragons, I killed one and the people gave me all this gold to say thank you. Now, I'm tired after my travels and I think I need a bath."

Matthew scooped the gold coins back into the bag. He stood up and strode off along the street towards his home. "I'll tell everyone about my adventures later," he called over his shoulder. "I think I'll have a party to celebrate coming home, you're all invited, I'll see you all tonight at eight o'clock." With that, he waved and disappeared through his front door.

That night, the whole village came to marvel at Matthew's tales of mountains and monsters. They all gasped when he showed them the cloak, but they gasped even more when he opened the door to the kitchen and showed off the gold coins that were in neat piles on the table.

When everyone had gone home, Matthew sat talking with his parents. "Well son, I have to say I'm really proud of you," his dad said. "Although I was a bit upset to see the mess you'd made of that cloak. It took me ages to find leather of the right quality."

"Yes dad, I'm sorry. Still, I can afford to buy you new leather now should I need a new cloak."

"I hope you'll *not* be needing a new cloak," his mother said. "I think you've done enough gallivanting for now."

"Yes, all right mother. I think my meeting with the Granscher has been enough of an adventure."

Matthew settled quickly back to ordinary life. He had a small house built which used up half of his gold. He started a vegetable garden. He had tea parties with his friends, and the children of the village wanted to hear the story of the Granscher over and over. Matthew was very content – for a while.

The autumn set in, and then the winter, and he enjoyed his life of comfort and his standing as a local celebrity. However, when the spring came, the local children began to pester him.

"When are you setting off on another journey?"

"Where are you going?"

"What other monsters are you going to defeat?"

When Matthew said that he was happy living a settled life, the children were very disappointed, and, being children, they told him so.

The children's reaction unsettled Matthew. He was not so content now, he was still quite rich but he was a bit cross that his fame and celebrity status had not seemed to last as long as his bag of gold. His mother noticed the change.

"What's the matter son?" she asked one day when Matthew had come round for lunch.

"I don't know," Matthew moaned. "I don't seem to have as many visitors as before. And people ignore me in the street now. Before the winter festival people noticed when I was coming and you could see them nudging each other. Now, they just nod and say good morning. Oh mother, I think I've become ordinary!"

"There's nothing wrong with being ordinary Matthew, it's good enough for most folk."

"Well it's not good enough for me," Matthew snapped and he walked out of the kitchen and went back to his own house. His mother shook her head, but said nothing and left him alone.

One Thursday, Matthew was sitting having tea on his own. He was feeling rather low and was still wondering what had gone wrong. He decided that he needed to rekindle the interest, he would have to do something to bring back the feeling of being special.

"I need to go on another adventure," he told the empty chair opposite him. "But a less dangerous one than meeting the Granscher I hope."

Being rather impulsive, he put down his teacup and went to the fireplace. He took down the leather cloak that had been displayed on the wall. Then he rummaged in the cupboard and found his red leather bag. He stuffed some essentials into the bag: food, a knife, a plate and drinking cup, clean socks and so on. Then he put on his best walking boots, and set off without a word to anyone, not even his mother.

In a few days, Matthew had walked many miles and was in a part of the forest that was completely unknown to him. As he walked along a track, he was whistling quietly to himself. Then a robin sang sweetly from the top of a tree as if it was answering his whistle. Matthew stopped and listened to the sounds of the forest: a blackbird was turning over the leaf litter looking for worms, there was a croak like a rusty gate and a whirring flutter as a pheasant flew up into a tree, a woodpecker was drumming some way off, and then ... Matthew could hear a soft crying sound. Very quietly, he crept forward until he saw someone. A girl, about the same age as himself, was standing by a tree.

"She must be a princess," Matthew thought to himself because the girl was wearing a very expensive looking dress and she had a tiara in her hair that sparkled in the morning sunshine. "OK Matthew," he chuckled to himself. "It looks like you're about to have another adventure that will make the villagers sit up and take notice." He walked forward. "Good morning your highness," (Matthew had been brought up most carefully and he knew how to address people properly.) "Is everything all right?"

The girl spun round and there was a look of surprise and desperation on her tear stained face. It was then that Matthew saw the rope, it went round the girl's waist like a belt, but it also went round her wrists and then round the tree.

"What on earth is going on?" Matthew asked. "Who has tied you up? Do you need rescuing?" he asked rather too eagerly.

"Oh kind sir," the girl pleaded and she fell to her knees. But then she looked over her shoulder as if something terrible might be coming out of the dense undergrowth and she turned back to Matthew. "You must run away as quickly as you can, or Gerble will eat you as well as me!"

"Who or what –" Matthew's question was cut short by a horrible creaking and hissing, and then the question was answered for him as a huge spider-like creature dragged itself down the path towards him. Its body was in two segments. The bloated rear part, larger than a horse but a sickly green colour, was held off the ground by eight legs that came from the smaller front part. Each leg was as thick as a man's leg, but made of three jointed segments that made them twice as long as Matthew was tall. It was these joints that made the creaking sound as the creature lurched forward. There was a face on the front with five eyes and two fearsome looking fangs.

Matthew was petrified, he stood there unable to move, unable to speak.

"How deliciousss," the creature hissed. "Two sssnacksss for Gerble to sssuck on. How generousss of the villagersss."

The girl let out a piercing scream that cut through Matthew's terror. He tried throwing his tattered leather cloak at the creature to cover its five eyes, but one of the legs shot out surprisingly quickly and brushed it aside. Oh how Matthew wished that his parents had given him a sword or, better still, a bow and arrow so that he could fight the thing from a safer distance.

He wasn't sure why or what he was going to do, but he jumped between the girl and the terrible creature. As he did so, he fumbled about to untie the bag strings, reached in and searched for his knife. He yelped as his fingers found several of the Granscher scales that were still in the bottom of the bag. He clutched a handful of them and pulled his hand out. Several small cuts had opened up on his fingers. The smell of the blood seemed to excite the monster and it let out a hideously long hiss that sounded somehow very happy.

"Take that you vile thing!" Matthew shouted as he threw a Granscher scale at the monster. It flew with a whizz and cut into the front leg. The monster's hiss changed tone, the legs straightened and lifted the huge body high above the path.

"Watch out for the web!" screamed the girl. "She's going to tangle you in her web."

Gerble's green abdomen swung down and Matthew could see little spouts on the underside. Suddenly, jets of liquid shot out from the spouts but the liquid changed to glistening strings almost instantly and the web strands, each about as thick as a finger, squiggled their way towards Matthew. Automatically, he put up his hands to defend himself and, by pure luck, some Granscher scales were sticking out between his fingers. The scales sparkled and flashed and their sharp edges sliced through the first lengths of web which dropped to the ground like so many sticky sausages.

"You sssneaky little beassst! I'll trusss you up and sssavour your juisssesss for my sssupper!" Gerble hissed malevolently. The spouts shot out more and more sticky web, but Matthew managed to use the scales to slice them into harmless lengths scattered about the forest floor.

Gerble became more and more angry, and squirted more and more web. As she did so, she began to shrink! The more web she produced, the more resources the monster's body was using up to produce the web. The piles of sticky web pieces became thinner and thinner as she became smaller and smaller. Even when she was too small to make the web reach Matthew, she continued in a total rage, making web that coiled on the ground between her legs.

Eventually, she shrank to the size of a common, if slightly large, house spider. In the end, exhaustion made her stop; she lay there giving out tiny panting sounds.  Matthew walked over and was about to stamp on her when the girl called out plaintively.

"Oh, please don't."

"Why on earth shouldn't I?  That thing was going to eat us both…"  Matthew paused for a moment.  "Hold on, why *was* it going to eat you?  Why were you tied up here?  What is going on here?"

"It's a complicated story," said the girl.  She explained that the monster, Gerble, had threatened to destroy the whole village if she wasn't fed regularly.  Several men had died trying to destroy the filthy beast and, in the end, it had been decided that they would draw lots every three months to choose who would be sacrificed to save the rest of the village.

"I see," said Matthew.  "I've heard stories like that before, and then a knight in shining armour comes along, destroys the monster and gets to marry the princess as a reward, that's great!"

"Er, except, I'm not a princess… I'm the butcher's daughter."

"But what about the fine dress and the tiara?"  Matthew sounded rather disappointed.

"Well, as you can imagine, being chosen is not a great thing, but the villagers dress you up to make you feel special, to make you think it's an honour being picked to save the village.  Well, I can tell you, it doesn't work!" the girl said sullenly.  "Watch out!  She's escaping!"

Matthew whirled round and the spider was dragging itself away wearily, but it was stumbling and tripping over the tangle of web.  Matthew bent down and picked it up.  A tiny terrified voice begged for mercy.

"Please don't kill it," the girl begged again.

"But it was just going to eat us, and it sounded like it was going to enjoy doing so!"

"I know, but it can't do any harm now, and it's unlucky to kill a spider."

Matthew looked at the spider and, he wasn't sure, but it looked as if there was dampness around its five eyes.  Being soft-hearted, and hoping to impress the girl, he decided not to kill the spider.  Instead, he took out the drinking cup he had in his bag and put the spider in.  He was wondering what to do to keep it in the cup when he looked at the pieces of web scattered on the floor.  He picked one up, it was rubbery and stretchy.  As he pulled on it, it stretched out and went like a sheet of thin skin.  He stretched the skin of web across the top of the cup and trapped the spider inside.

"It'll suffocate in there, poor thing," the girl whined.

Matthew was beginning to be just a little bit annoyed with this girl who was supposed to be swooning at the feet of her brave rescuer.  He thought for a moment, but then used the teeth of one of the Granscher scales to make some tiny air holes.

"What about me?" the girl complained.  "I'm suffocating with this rope round my waist."

"Oh, sorry, here, let me help you."  Matthew used a Granscher scale to cut the rope.  Unfortunately, he snagged the girl's dress as he did so.

"Watch out," she shouted. "I want to keep this lovely dress to get married in, it's the only nice thing I've got, my dad's a useless butcher and he doesn't make enough money to buy me nice things."

"I bet your dad was really upset when your name was picked." Then, with a hint of exasperation, he muttered, "Or did he think it was his lucky day?"

"What do you mean?"

"It doesn't matter," Matthew smiled unconvincingly. "We'd better get you back to your father. Which way is the village?"

"Isn't it obvious," the girl said with contempt in her voice. "It's down that path." She bustled off muttering and trying to repair the pulled thread that Matthew had snagged with the Granscher scale. Matthew peered into the cup and an awful thought went through his mind, had he actually done the right thing in saving this ungrateful girl. He shrugged his shoulders, popped the cup into his bag, rescued his cloak from a nearby bush and set off after the girl. Then, another thought came into his head and he stopped.

"You never know, they might come in useful," he said to himself. He turned round, went back and collected up several handfuls of the web pieces. They had lost their stickiness, but they were still rubbery. He dropped them into the bag.

"Are you coming or not!" the girl shouted back rudely.

Matthew thought for a few moments. The villagers were bound to be grateful, there might be another reward of gold, but, then again, the butcher was poor. On a positive note, if the stories were to be believed, he would marry the girl and then he would have someone to cook his dinner and keep his house clean while he looked after his vegetable garden and entertained his admirers. But, then again, she was certainly no princess and decidedly grumpy besides.

By now, the girl was out of sight, but he could still hear her moaning about something. Without another thought, Matthew turned again and walked very quickly – back in the direction from which he had first come, back towards his own home!

## Chapter 3 – DISAPPOINTMENT

"Well Matthew Sadler," he was talking to himself as he journeyed home. "That's another fine adventure you've completed." He peered into his bag. "Shame there's no treasure, but I've defeated another monster, and I'm actually bringing it home, the kids'll be wowed."

As is usual for young people, Matthew was very concerned about appearing to be grown up and he began to wonder about his name.

"Matthew's a bit young," he mused to himself one evening while sitting by his camp fire. "I think Matt sounds more… more relaxed, more nonchalant (he was actually very well educated). That's it, I'll call myself Matt from now on, Matthew and my childhood have passed into history, the stuff of legends." He smiled to himself, wrapped himself in his cloak and settled contentedly to sleep.

There was a great stir in his home village when Matt was spotted coming down the road. Children and dogs ran up the hill to greet him with excited questions, yaps and yelps.

"Where have you been?"

"What's in the bag this time?"

"Have you got lots of gold?"

"Did you kill another monster?"

All this mixed in with dogs jumping up, growling at each other and making a terrible din. The adults looked up from their gardens or came out of their houses to see what all the fuss was about.

"He's back," Matthew's father called excitedly through the window. Mrs Sadler came rushing out of the house wiping the dough from her hands. She stood by the gate, admiring her son as he strode down the hill. Matt smiled and waved, but kept walking at the same pace, determined to show how mature he was now. When he finally reached the gate, his mother wrapped her arms around him and tears of joy burst out.

"Oh mother," he huffed. "Don't get flour on my cloak." He was very proud of its weather-stained look and the holes and scratches, he thought it made a real statement about him being a hero.

"Where in heaven's name have you been?" she scolded. "You just disappeared without saying a word, I've been sick with worry. You're such a naughty boy!"

"Mother, I'm not a little boy any more, I'm grown up, I've been on adventures, I've defeated two monsters, I've got enough gold to last me the rest of my life!" Matt held his mother at arm's length and looked rather cross. Her face crumpled and her tears flowed even more freely.

"I'm sorry Matthew," she wailed. "But to me, you'll always be my little boy, and I was sure something terrible had happened to you. I didn't know if you had been kidnapped, or had an accident, or what –"

"Oh mother," he interrupted rather sheepishly. "I'm sorry, but I just felt that I needed to go on another adventure. By the way, I call myself Matt now, it's more, sort of, well – anyway, I want to be called Matt from now on."

Now his father stepped forward and shook Matt's hand stiffly. "Welcome back son, er – Matt," he said awkwardly. They went inside while the children crowded round the door and peered in through the open windows. The dogs wandered off to find something more interesting like a hole to dig or a bone to gnaw.

"Come on you lot, off about your business," his father called.

"Oh, they're doing no harm," Matt said, smiling at the children. "They're bound to be interested, they want to hear about my adventures."

"I'm not sure *I* do, but I bet you would love a nice cup of tea," his mother said and she went to the kitchen to put the kettle on. Matt began rummaging in his red leather bag.

"Have you got more gold Matthew?" a cheeky freckle-faced little girl asked from the doorway.

"My name is Matt if you don't mind. In any case, I've already collected enough gold from my adventure with the Granscher," Matt boasted. "I've brought back something much more interesting this time… Gerble web." He pulled out a piece of the web and tossed it playfully at the girl. She caught it but, when it squirmed and wobbled in her hand, she screamed, threw it on the floor and ran away wailing that Matthew was being horrible to her. The other children backed away at first, but then one or two of the braver ones edged forward.

"It won't hurt you," Matt laughed. He pulled out another piece and started playing with it, stretching it and bouncing it on the floor. Little Lennie picked up the piece by the door.

"Ooh, it's weird," he giggled as he squeezed it. "It's full of rainbows. What is it? What's Gerble web?"

"It's a piece of the web of a giant spider," Matt answered with a leer. Lennie screamed and dropped the web. The other children laughed at him but none of them went near the glistening lump that lay in the doorway.

"You're kidding," someone said. "There ain't no such thing as giant spiders; they're just in the stories children get told round the fire to frighten them and keep them from going out into the forest." Sarah Alport pushed to the front, a hint of a sneer on her face. "They're like ogres and goblins, spooks to scare the babies."

"Do you believe in the Granscher, Sarah?" Matt asked coolly. "You've seen my cloak, you've seen the scales, and you've seen the gold." All the children nodded, Matt had told them the tale and shown them his trophies on lots of occasions. "Well, Gerble the giant spider is just as real, and," his voice rose grandly, "I rescued a princess who was going to be eaten by the filthy beast." He leaned forward to emphasise the drama. "She nearly ate me!"

"What, the princess nearly ate you?" Sarah laughed, and so did the other children.

"Oh, very funny. No, Gerble nearly ate me," he said dramatically as he stood up and raised his hands like two spiders. "She had huge poisonous fangs and, when she pulled her vile green body up to its full height on her eight long, spiky legs, she was as tall as this house!" The children all gasped, they gasped again when Matt's mother dropped the tea tray in the kitchen with a loud crash.

"Oh, my good Lord! My poor little boy!" she wailed. Matt looked embarrassed.

"Wh-what happened to Gerble?" Lennie asked nervously.

"I've got her in here," Matt said as he put his hand back into the bag. Most of the children screamed and started to run away.

"Hold on," said Sarah with her defiant hands on her hips. The others all stopped. "How can a giant spider fit in that little bag?"

Matt told the children to come in and sit down. It was just like old times, he had an audience again, he was special again, and he loved the feeling. He continued the story of how he had defeated and captured Gerble. Of course, he exaggerated details and, in his version, the slicing of the web was intentional not a stroke of luck.

"So, why didn't you marry the princess?" Sarah asked. "That's what you're supposed to do."

Matt looked around the room while he thought. "She wasn't as pretty as some of the girls in this village." One or two of the older girls blushed shyly, hoping that no one was looking at them.

"Okay, but why didn't you bring back any gold from the princess' father, he must have wanted to give you a reward?" Lennie asked.

Matt had a quick coughing fit to cover his confusion, but it didn't take him long to gather himself. "I've… I've already got more gold than I need," he boasted. "I told the king, because of course the princess' father was a great king. I told the king to use the gold to set up a charity in my name to help poor children."

"Huh," snorted Sarah. "You could have brought it back and given it to us. We're poor, well, some of the children in the village are." She looked straight at Lennie, and he looked down at the floor. "Anyway, where is this spider, this Gerble?"

Matt took his cup out of the red leather bag and peeled back the stretched web. He showed it to Sarah first, hoping to impress or scare her. She was made of sterner stuff, she put her hand straight in the cup and picked Gerble out. Several children backed away, but others took a closer look. Lennie began to giggle, others joined in.

"She's not very scary," mocked Sarah.

"Well not now that I've tamed her," Matt said angrily. "You *would* have been scared if you had met her when she was as big as a house. Even I was a *bit* frightened."

"Well, if you say so. Oh, look at the time, I really must go home for my tea." Sarah dropped the spider back into the cup, turned and just walked out. Matt was devastated. He shooed all the children away, gathered up his things, and stomped to his old bedroom.

"Don't you want some tea, Matthew my love?" his mother bleated.

"Leave me alone, and my name is Matt, Matt the man who has adventures and conquers monsters!" he snapped as his door slammed.

## Chapter 4 – THE TRAP

"Stupid kids, what do they know?" Matt was back in his own house, sat slumped against the wall bouncing a piece of Gerble web dejectedly against the opposite wall and catching it again. Nobody except his mother had been to visit for three days.

"Well love, it's not really their fault." As always, his mother could see both sides. "I'm not surprised that the village found a little spider in a pot and a lump of rubbery stuff less impressive than a bag of dragon scales and gold. I mean to say…"

"Not you as well!" Matt snapped. "You've no idea what I've been through. Oh… why do I bother? Haven't you got some washing or… dusting or something to do!" He snatched at the piece of web, stood up and stalked off to his bedroom, slamming the door behind him. His mother shook her head, but left quietly.

Meanwhile, Gerble had escaped from the cup and had spun a delicate web in the corner of the room. She was sucking happily on a juicy house spider that had walked into her web, and, if you looked very carefully, she had grown a tiny bit…

In his room, Matt lay on the bed for hours just staring at the ceiling, reliving all the things he had seen and done since being presented with the leather cloak by his proud father.

Suddenly, he jumped to his feet and looked at himself in the mirror. "Come on Matt," he said to himself pulling a stern face. "You're a man of action.  You'll have to show these stop-at-home wimps what life is really about."

With that, he jumped up, grabbed the cloak and bag that had been thrown scornfully into the corner of the room three days earlier, and marched out into the street.  Some children were playing hopscotch and, although they were not paying him any attention, Matt announced, "I'm off on another adventure, goodbye!"

The children looked for a moment, and then carried on playing.  Matt threw the cloak round his shoulders extravagantly, lifted his chin, and strode off out into the forest.

Several days later, Matt was walking along a forest path when he realised that he couldn't hear anything, there were no birds singing, not even a cricket chirping.  Then he caught sight of the top of a tower above the trees ahead of him.  As he went forward, the trees thinned to bushy scrub, and then he came into a large clearing.  The ground was bare, there was no grass and there were no flowers, just grey soil that looked as if it had been wasted by fire.  In the middle of the clearing stood a tall tower made of rough, black rock.

Matt was tired and fed up with walking through the forest; he needed a wash and would have liked to sit at a table to eat a good meal.  More than that, he really wanted to talk with another human being, and so he crossed the clearing and banged his fist on the great, nail-studded door at the foot of the tower.  The door wasn't actually closed and it swung open silently with the weight of the banging. Matt peered in cautiously.

The ground floor of the tower was one huge circular chamber with a neat stone flagged floor and a very high, white ceiling. There were two high backed chairs and a table at one side near a large, smoke stained hearth, but there was no fire in the grate. There were no windows, but the room was lit dimly by a lamp hanging from the centre of the ceiling. Opposite the fireplace was a flight of stone steps that curled around the wall and disappeared through a hole in the ceiling. Directly below the hole in the ceiling, there was a hole in the floor and it looked as if another set of steps went down from the room.

"Er, is - is - anyone home?" Matt called. He knocked again on the door and the sound boomed around the cavernous room. He took a few steps in from the door when, suddenly, a fire burst into life in the hearth and a hand appeared above the back of one of the chairs. It was beckoning Matt to come in. He gulped and turned to run, but the door slammed shut. He grappled with the handle, but it wouldn't open.

"Oh, don't go, I've been waiting for you." The voice was surprisingly soft, it was a child's voice. Matt felt reassured and took a few more steps into the room. Then a tall girl with long black hair stood up from the chair.

"Sarah? Sarah Alport? What are you doing here? Why aren't you back in the village? How did you get here? Where *is* here? Whose tower is this? What is going on?" The questions tumbled from his lips giving Sarah no chance to answer.

"Slow down, slow down," she said in a voice that somehow made Matt remember how tired he was. "Come and rest, you've had a long journey. I've made some tea for you, come and sit down."

Matt's legs felt suddenly heavy, he felt really sleepy; he needed desperately to sit down. He dragged himself over to the chair by the fire. There was a gold tea set: teapot, cups, saucers and a plate of small cakes on the table. Almost in slow motion, he leaned forward, took a cup and sipped the sweet liquid, but it wasn't tea, it tasted of blackberries. He felt an irresistible urge to curl up and sleep.

When he awoke, Matt found himself in a cold, circular chamber with a damp, earth floor and a dark, stone vaulted ceiling. He could hear water running. There was a dim light coming from a hole at the edge of the ceiling. A set of steps clung to the wall as they spiralled down from the hole, but they stopped half way down and the bottom step was out of reach. When he looked around in the gloom, Matt could just make out a small stream flowing across the middle of the floor and disappearing through a grating on the far side of the chamber. He didn't know how much time he had been asleep but he felt very hungry and there was a dent in the earth floor where he had been laying. He struggled to sit himself up, he was very stiff.

"What the-?"

"Ah, he's awake," a sharp voice came down from above. The light dimmed even more as a figure appeared at the hole.  It was an old woman, thin and tall but bent over as if she had been carrying a heavy burden all her life.  "Good day to you, Matthew Sadler, I hope you slept well."  The voice had no hint of warmth or welcome in it.

Somewhere deep inside, Matt felt a flicker of bravery.  "My name's Matt, I left Matthew behind on one of my adventures!  Who are you?  What is happening?  Where am I?"  Then an unselfish thought came into his mind.  "What have you done with Sarah?"

"Oh, so many questions," cackled the old hag.  "Let me see, I'll answer them in reverse order.  Sarah?  She has gone back into your memory, that's where I found her.  It was rather nice taking on a younger shape for a while, I wish I could do it permanently; these old bones do so feel the cold and damp.  Sarah obviously means something to you, you were thinking about her as you walked through the forest.  You seem to want to impress her but your memory didn't tell me why."  Matt felt his cheeks warm as he blushed.  "Ah, now I see why, now I see what drives you, you just want to be famous, Matt Sadler the great adventurer."  There was a nasty jeer and the figure spat at Matt.

"You vile old woman!"

"Oh, I know," she said proudly.  "You asked where you are; well you are in my dungeon.  And what is happening?"  The voice now seethed with venom.  "I am punishing you, I am going to leave you to rot and die, slowly."  The last word was drawn out and really savoured.

"But why?" Matt pleaded.

"My last answer should tell you," the voice was rising to a shriek. "Who am I? I am the Granscher's mother! The Granscher was my creation, you destroyed my child!" she screamed. "Now I am going to destroy you, but I am going to cause you as much suffering as I have endured since that terrible day when I felt the stab of my child's death pierce my heart!" With that, she turned and dragged herself up the stairs sobbing bitterly.

Matt slumped against the dungeon wall in despair. But, as cold, hungry and frightened as he felt, he drifted off to sleep.

As the days passed, Matt explored his prison, looking for some way to escape. There was no way that he could jump to reach the lowest step of the incomplete stairway and the wall was too slimy to climb. The grating where the stream escaped looked the most obvious way out, but it wouldn't move and the rock in which it was set was too smooth and hard to scratch away, even with a Granscher scale.

From time to time, the Granscher's mother would appear on the steps to taunt him. Matt slumped beneath the stairs so that she couldn't see him. He was dejected and downhearted, there was no way out, he was doomed. He thought of the children playing happily in the village sunshine, he longed for the safety of home.

"Why did I have to come on another adventure?" he said bitterly.

Matt pulled a piece of the Gerble web from his bag and began squeezing and bouncing it. This seemed to comfort him. He imagined he was back in his house and threw the rubbery lump against the wall opposite and it bounced back. He threw it again, but it didn't come back, it stuck in the grating where the stream gurgled out of the dungeon. Matt dragged himself across to retrieve the piece of web. Where the stream had splashed the web, it had swollen up to twice its original size.

An idea flashed into Matt's brain, could that be a way out? Frantically, he rummaged in his bag, pulled out the pieces of web and stuffed them into the holes in the grating. As the grating was blocked, the stream began to back up. Matt had to wade in to block the last holes, the icily cold water made him catch his breath.

Very quickly, the stream spread across the floor of the dungeon, then it was ankle deep, then knee deep. Matt wrapped his leather cloak around to keep out the worst of the chill, but cold wet fingers found their way in through the rips made by the Granscher's dying struggles. However, the leather retained enough air pockets to help Matt float as the water became deeper. Steadily, the cold, dark water rose, and so did Matt. Eventually, he was able to grab onto the bottom step of the stone staircase. He hauled himself out and lay cold and exhausted. His bag drifted past and Matt snatched it from the black pool. The water continued to rise and so he climbed silently towards the light coming down from the hole in the ceiling.

Matt put his head warily up into the room with the hearth and the stone flagged floor. The fire was burning brightly and the gold tea set was on the table, but there was no sign of his jailer in the chair. Matt made a run for the door. He struggled with the handle. It wouldn't turn. He plunged his hand into his bag and pulled out a Granscher scale. He tore frantically at the door with the scale, trying to cut through the thick timber.

A hand clamped onto his shoulder. He spun round. As he turned, the jagged edge of the scale caught the arm that was gripping him. The Granscher's mother screamed with a mixture of rage and pain. Matt's arms flailed desperately to beat off his attacker. Each time the scale bit into her hands or arms, the Granscher's mother shrieked and leapt back. It was as if some of her vicious magic was concentrated in the scales and was being returned to her. But she was not going to give up, she kept coming back, driven by pure hatred.

Slashing with one hand, Matt struggled with the other to find more scales in his bag until he had three or four held between each finger of his clenched fists. Then he went on the attack. Jabbing out with his armoured fists, he moved forward and his enemy, obviously terrified of the remains of her own child that were now turned against her, backed away. Matt felt bolder and his spirit was rekindled, he let out an angry roar and rushed at the Granscher's mother, pushing her right across the chamber. She was in a blind panic, flapping and scratching to fend off Matt's assault.

Then she stumbled and fell back into the fire. There was a vivid green flash and a screech as her clothes flared and then a moan as she seemed to melt. She slumped into the hearth and pools of a black liquid ran out from beneath her and dribbled down between the stones. Soon, there was nothing left and the fire died.

Matt collapsed in an exhausted heap and drifted off into a sleep that was far deeper than any he had endured in the previous few days.

When he awoke, Matt looked around. There was a pile of grey ash in the hearth and a black stain where the liquid had been. Matt clambered to his feet and gathered up all the Granscher scales that had scattered on the floor when the fight had finished. He made for the door, but then remembered the gold tea set. "That will impress the real Sarah," he thought to himself. When he turned round, he was shocked to see that the tea set was a dull grey colour.

He picked up the pot, it was very heavy, it seemed to be made of a metal like lead. He gave it a funny look, but shrugged and dropped the tea set piece by piece into his bag and it made a series of dreary thuds. There was a bag of dry leaves on the table. It looked like tea but, when he smelled it, Matt recognised the flavour of the drink that had put him to sleep. "That might come in handy," he said to himself. He put the small bag into his red shoulder bag. He thought about eating the cake, but then thought it might not be a good idea. He wrapped his cloak around his shoulders and went back to the door.

The door opened easily and Matt blinked as he stepped out into the sunshine. How the scene had changed. He could hear birds singing, and he could smell sweet nectar as butterflies flitted between the flowers that now carpeted the clearing around the tower.

A bramble was growing against the tower wall, it was studded with glistening blackberries. Matt reached forward but then stopped. As hungry as he was, he was scared to eat them. Then a bird flew down, cocked its head to look at Matt, and then it pecked and swallowed three of the blackberries and flew away. Matt still hesitated, but then he gave in to his hunger. He lunged forward, grabbed a handful of the juicy fruits and stuffed them into his mouth. He sighed with pleasure as cool juice slid across his tongue and dribbled down his chin. The taste was heavenly, sugary but sharp. When he had picked and eaten all the ripe blackberries, he looked around trying to remember the direction home.

"That's enough adventuring for you, Matt Sadler" he said to himself. "Time to go home, and this time to stay." Still tired, but feeling very good, Matt set off back along the path that he thought had brought him to the tower. He began whistling a cheerful tune as he walked. Behind him, he heard a low sigh. He looked back briefly. "Just the wind blowing past the empty tower," he said to a lizard basking on a rock beside him. Matt shook his head and walked into the forest.

## Chapter 5 – LORD STERMIAN

Matt was tired and the clearing around the tower had looked completely different, so it was not surprising that he set off in the wrong direction. After several days of walking through the forest, when he expected to be back in familiar surroundings, Matt was puzzled to see hills in the distance. There were no hills near his home village. He carried on, hoping to find civilisation.

After two more days walking along seemingly endless forest tracks, he saw smoke rising above the trees and he turned towards it. The forest track he was following became wider and, eventually, he came to a village. The houses were not like the neat, timber-framed and white-washed cottages with golden thatch of his own village. They were very small, built of yellow brick with red tiled roofs, and they were in a terrible state. The windows had no glass but ramshackle wooden shutters, paint was peeling from the doors, broken fences struggled to contain the weeds that choked the small front gardens.

As Matt walked down the tatty street, a woman came out of one of the houses. She was dressed in rags, her hair straggled wildly and her face looked grey.

"Good morning," Matt chirped. "Lovely day isn't it."

"If you say so, sir," the woman replied in a dreary voice but she didn't look up.

"I have been travelling for many days, is there an inn where I can clean myself up, buy food and rest my weary feet?" Matt was trying to be cheerful, but the surroundings made it difficult.

"We don't have an inn," the woman almost moaned. Still she looked down at the ground. "We couldn't afford to spend money at an inn. It's hard enough being able to feed ourselves after paying all the taxes without wasting money on ale. Still, we try to do the right thing here, you are welcome to rest in my humble home and I can share some food with you. Come in." The woman turned back to her dilapidated front door.

"That's very kind of you," but Matt hung back, not sure he wanted to enter the house.

"Come on, come on," the woman insisted. Matt gave in and followed her. The inside of the house was much as he had expected; old yellowed whitewash was flaking from the walls, the floor was bare boards, ragged curtains hung at the windows. The only furniture was a rickety chair and table. A wooden platter, an old leather jug and a spoon and cup made from horn were the only items on the table, and there was no sign of a cupboard that might contain other domestic items. In one corner of the room was a pile of straw with an old blanket thrown over. A pile of ash and embers smoked in the hearth, a single black pot stood nearby.

"I'm sorry I don't have ale or meat, but you are welcome to a drink of water and some gruel." The woman had a sad voice, but it was touched with kindness. "What is your name?"

"Matt, Matt Sadler, and yours?"

"I am called Sarah, sir." The coincidence struck Matt and he thought of how different this Sarah's nature was compared to Sarah Alport, but he said nothing.

Sarah took the wooden platter to the pot, spooned out some lumpy sludge and returned to the table. Then she poured some water into the cup and offered Matt the chair. Reluctantly, he sat down and looked at the platter. He looked around the dismal room. There had been times when Matt complained to his parents that other children in his village had things that he didn't have, he made a mental note to be more grateful when he finally returned home.

"I know it doesn't look very appetising," Sarah apologised. "If you'd come last week, I had found some ripe blackberries growing in a forest clearing and that had been a real treat. But they're all gone now."

Matt began to feel really sorry for the poor woman, she really was far kinder than the other Sarah. "It's all right, I've had quite enough blackberries on my travels." Cautiously, he tasted the gruel, it was surprisingly good. He could feel the warm nourishment spreading through his body. He was about to ask for some more, but remembered that the spoon had been scraping the bottom of the pot when Sarah had been serving it. He looked around the room again. It was very shabby, but it was clean. Sarah's clothes were old and ragged, but they too were clean, as were her hands and careworn face.

Matt's heart softened even more towards the poor woman.

"This is delicious, you must give me the recipe for my mother." Matt saw a flush of pink spread across the woman's down turned face.

"You're too kind, sir."

"No," Matt said quietly. "*You* are kind. You have invited a stranger into your home and shared your food with him. I am glad there is no inn, I am pleased to be your guest. Here, take this." He slid his hand into the lining of his jacket where his money was sewn for security. He pulled out a small gold coin and put it on the table.

"Oh my gracious!" Sarah gasped. "I cannot take that, if Lord Stermian finds out that I have a gold coin he will be angry!" She looked terror stricken.

"Stermian? Who is Lord Stermian? Why would he be angry if you had a gold coin?"

"He is the lord who rules this land, and only he may have gold. It is rumoured that he has a whole palace made of gold. We, his people, have nothing; he bleeds us dry with taxes to pay for his extravagance. If he found out that I had a gold coin, he would have my poor humble house destroyed and I would be forced to live wild in the forest."

"That's terrible," Matt said angrily. "You a kind and decent woman, you deserve better. Your lord, Stermian did you say? He should be providing for his people not taking from them." A determined look came into his eye. "I will have to do something to help you, and the other people of your village."

"Oh no," cried Sarah desperately. "He has soldiers, he will have you killed."

"He can't be any more dangerous than the Granscher or Gerble." Matt puffed his chest out, but Sarah just looked bewildered. "They are monsters that I have conquered on my travels. I think I can handle a greedy lord." The old woman just kept shaking her head. "Where is this lord's palace?" Matt asked.

"I don't really know, I've only heard rumours of it. But a troop of Lord Stermian's men come round regularly to collect taxes. We have no money left, and so they take goods in kind, food that we have grown or things that we have made. Lord Stermian often accompanies his horrible men; he seems to gain pleasure from seeing how poor we are. You will meet him soon enough."

"I will wait for him."

"You are welcome to share my home, but I fear there will not be enough food for the two of us."

"Thank you again," Matt said. "But I cannot impose on you any more. I will camp at the edge of the village and find my own food. In the meantime, take these instead of the gold coin." He pulled the leaden tea set from his bag and presented it to the woman. Her face was a picture, to her, this was a great treasure.

"This is real pewter! Oh sir, I cannot accept this in payment for such a humble meal."

"That meal saved my life," Matt said rather pompously. "It was worth more to me than if the tea set was made of gold, indeed, it was worth more than

Lord Stermian's golden palace. And now, I must go and set up my camp."

Matt used his leather cloak to make a shelter at the edge of the village and he made himself comfortable. There was no sign of Lord Stermian or his soldiers for several days, but Matt waited patiently. He went off into the forest to hunt for food. The Granscher scales made wonderful arrow heads and also tools to make a bow. The few pieces of Gerble web he had left could be stretched to make snares as well as the bow string. During his travels, it had turned out that Matt was quite a successful hunter. Sarah and the other villagers all welcomed him and he visited each home in turn to share in their meagre but generous hospitality and supplement the food with fresh meat.

The longer he stayed, the more he learned about the harsh lives of the villagers. They were ashamed of the shabby state of their houses and gardens. They wished that they could paint the doors, glaze the windows and grow flowers in their gardens. Lord Stermian's tax demands were so ruthless that they had to spend every waking moment toiling in the fields or in their workshops, growing food or making things to hand over to the tax gatherers.

Matt was determined that these good people deserved better, he just wasn't sure what he was going to do when he met this Lord Stermian. "Still," he thought to himself. "My quick wits have got me through all my adventures so far. I'm sure I'll think of something when the moment arrives."

One morning, Matt was roused by the distant sound of hooves. All the villagers stumbled and scrambled out and stood by their doors looking terrified. Then a troop of mounted soldiers entered the village. They were dressed in black leather tabards over polished mail shirts. Each tabard had a large S on top of a flame circled sun emblazoned on the front and back in gold. Their heads and faces were covered by enclosed gold helmets that shone in the sunlight. In their midst, was a glorious golden coach that sparkled as it bounced along in the sunshine. It was pulled by four magnificent palomino horses with smooth golden flanks and flowing white manes. The harness jingled with gold fittings and ornaments. There was no doubt in Matt's mind that he was about to meet Lord Stermian.

"Good morning, peasants," one of the guards sneered at the poor villagers who all bowed and mumbled, "Good morning sir."

The guard dismounted. He was carrying a large bag and he walked towards them. "This month's tax will be one gold ducat per household," he said leaning forward until his mask was touching Sarah's face. His voice seethed with cruelty.

"But we have no gold ducats," wailed Sarah.

"I have." The guard whirled round to see Matt striding into the village. "I have enough gold coins to pay for each household." He flipped a gold coin and it glinted in the morning sunshine. The guard looked taken aback.

The door of the coach swung open and a tall figure stepped down. He was dressed from head to foot in gold embroidered cloth and a gold circlet held his long hair, which itself looked like fine spun gold, in place. Each finger and thumb had at least one gold ring, some had two or three. An intricate gold chain hung from his neck with a pendant in the shape of a blazing sun swinging heavily against his chest.

"Ah, Lord Stermian I presume." Matt bowed politely, remembering his mother's lessons on how to greet people appropriately if you wanted something from them. "Allow me to introduce myself, Matt, Matt Sadler at your service."

"Seize him!" Stermian hadn't had the benefits of Matt's good mannered upbringing.

"Hold on there!" Matt held up one hand. The guards were confused by his commanding manner, they were used to people being frightened of them. "I am Matt Sadler, adventurer, slayer of the mighty Granscher and nemesis to the great spider Gerble." He sounded so impressive that the guards all stopped, the villagers all looked at each other. Even Matt was rather surprised by himself. He wasn't sure where the words were coming from, but he felt good and so he carried on. "I do not have the gold with me, I prefer to travel light. However, if the good Lord Stermian will have tea with me, I will tell him where there is enough gold to build a new palace that will dwarf his present magnificent home."

Lord Stermian almost fell over in his rush to hear more. Matt was sure he saw a little dribble of desire on Stermian's chin as he approached.

"Join me in my humble travelling lodge." Matt waved his arm to indicate the leather cloak strung between two small trees. He turned to the villagers. "Good people, while Lord Stermian is my guest, will you entertain his troops to tea?" The looks on the villagers' faces were amazing. "Trust me good people, kindness will melt hard hearts." He winked at Sarah. "My good friend, I have some special tea, a fine blend that was given to me by the Granscher's mother herself when she entertained me at her tower. I have been saving it for a special occasion, and today is obviously such an occasion. Come to my shelter and I will share some with you." He turned and strutted back to his tent, Sarah followed, confused but excited.

Very quickly, Matt whispered and explained about the tea and warned Sarah not to let any of the villagers drink it. This instruction was unnecessary because the soldiers, when their Lord and the mysterious stranger were out of sight, grabbed the tea for themselves. When one of them found the tea set on Sarah's table, he waved it triumphantly and they all crammed into her tiny house and used it to make their own brew.

Sat by the shelter, Lord Stermian listened wide eyed to Matt's stories. Matt boiled water on the camp fire in a small pot given to him by one of the grateful villagers. He used a wooden ladle to stir in some of the leaves he had collected from the tower and the water flushed with golden glow. Lord Stermian thought the sweet smell was delicious.

"I'm sorry that I have not brought one of my gold cups for you to use but, as I said, I prefer to travel light and gold is *so* heavy," Matt apologised. "I do have a very special cup, however." Lord Stermian was impressed, until Matt brought out his simple horn cup. "It looks humble but the great Gerble herself has drunk from this cup."

Lord Stermian wasn't too sure, but he took the cup and his gold rings clinked against it side. Matt poured steaming liquid into the cup. Lord Stermian breathed in the fragrant aroma.

"This is not like the tea that we have in these parts, but it is such a lovely golden colour," Lord Stermian drooled and he took a careful sip. "Oh, that is so delicious, it makes me feel happy, and cosy and..." His eyelids drooped, his chin sank down onto his chest and, in a very few moments, Lord Sermian was snoring quietly, unaware of the hot liquid that had spilled on his lap as he dropped the cup.

Very soon, the villagers had Lord Stermian and his troops tied up in the middle of the village. They used the reins from Stermian's coach harness. They were all congratulating Matt and each other.

"What shall we do with them?" someone asked.

"That's up to you," said Matt. "But I would suggest that you do not untie them, never give your enemies a second chance. Perhaps, if you spread the word to other villages in this land, the people will realise that they have the strength to control a tyrant such as Lord Stermian, he is, after all, only one man and they are many."

Matt was sitting in Lord Stermian's coach running his hands over the gold upholstery. "Sarah Alport would've been impressed with this." He smiled to himself and then climbed out.

Old Sarah came up to him. "Good morning Matt. We have been talking amongst ourselves. You have been so kind, we would like you to be our new lord. We would be quite happy to see you riding in the gold coach."

"As I said before Sarah, it is you and the other villagers who have been kind. I think you deserve the coach."

"Oh good gracious no," she shook her head.

"Perhaps not to ride in, but to break up and share out, to return what is rightfully yours. I'm sure I would have loved to ride home in such a coach when I was younger, but I'm older and hopefully wiser now. I'm not sure I want all the attention that it would bring."

Something inside told Matt that he needed to leave, that he needed to get home. Of course, all the villagers asked him to stay.

"No, no, I really must go. I've found a map in Stermian's coach and it shows me the way back to West Fennyland."

Matt packed his red leather bag, wrapped himself in his tattered, leather cloak and waved goodbye to the villagers. There was a tear in Sarah's eye, and Matt had a slightly misty view of the path ahead as he set off. Then something struck him, he had not collected anything from his adventure that might prove useful in the future. "Does that mean I won't be having anymore adventures?" he thought to himself.

"Matt, Matt, wait!" It was Sarah trying to run as fast as her old legs would carry her. "Matt, if you must go, why walk? Why not take one of Lord Stermian's beautiful horses, he won't be needing them any more and we are not going on any long journeys."

"But I cannot ride, and besides, there is no saddle."

"We will teach you."

Matt smiled and turned back. He didn't really need much of an excuse to stay, but something was still nagging inside, calling him to go home.

Matt was a quick learner and he soon mastered the horses. One in particular stood out, it was slightly larger, it held its head proudly while the others were slightly browbeaten. Lord Stermian had treated his horses cruelly, and Matt's kinder approach soon had the beautiful beast literally eating out of his hand. As for a saddle, the guards had all ridden into the village and so there were plenty of saddles to choose from. And so, one week later, Matt again said his farewells but, this time, he rode off into the forest. Lord Stermian and his men were still slumped snoring in the street bound tightly with the gold chased leather reins of the coach harness.

## Chapter 6 – HOMEWARD

Matt rode through the forest at a gentle pace. This seemed to please the horse which had been used to hauling Lord Stermian's heavy, golden coach through the land at a speed intended to frighten the population. In a moment of silliness, Matt named the horse G-G after Granscher and Gerble, but G-G was far more placid than either of the two monsters.

The sun was shining, robins were still singing from treetops. The forest was at its most beautiful as summer was passing into autumn and the leaves were turning to a rainbow of reds, purples and yellows. Matt came to one broad hornbeam tree which had scattered a lot of its leaves on the ground. In the sunlight, it looked as if the forest floor was scattered with gold coins. As there was no one else about, Matt spoke gently to the horse.

"What would Lord Stermian make of such a glorious sight, eh G-G? He'd probably burst a blood vessel with desire rushing around trying to collect all the gold."

"No, he'd stand and watch his servants do the collecting for him."

Matt nearly fell from the saddle, G-G could speak!

"Wh- wh-" he spluttered.

"Oh, I'm so sorry, did I startle you?" G-G said in a beautifully cultured voice that was like velvet being stroked.

"B- but you can talk. You're a horse, but you can talk!" Matt was amazed. "How come you can talk?

Why have you kept quiet so far? Why didn't you speak before?"

"As kind as you have been, I wasn't sure that I could trust you. Lord Stermian treated me very badly; I needed to be sure that you really were as good as you seemed to be. I come from a very long and distinguished line of horses. I can trace my ancestors back to a time when the world was very different. Some of them could actually fly as well as talk. I know that some of my family were ill-used by humans when it was discovered that they could talk. They were used as entertainment in circuses and shows. I am sure that, if he had known, Lord Stermian would have used me in some unscrupulous way to increase his store of gold. I had to be certain that you would respect me."

"I *thought* there was something different about you, you seemed to have a special air about you."

"Thank you," G-G said modestly.

"Do you mind being ridden?"

"I loathed pulling the cart of that awful man." G-G's dismissive word for what Lord Sermian thought was a magnificent coach summed up his nobility. "I am quite happy to carry you, you are a true man." The compliment made Matt sit straighter and pride swelled his chest.

The two fellow travellers continued their journey, telling each other tales of their adventures. G-G's stories of her ancestors enthralled Matt and made him feel rather humble about his own escapades. Even when the autumn weather turned, he was happy to ride in the heavy rain because G-G just ignored it and walked on at her stately pace.

Lord Stermian's map showed a river bordering his land with Matt's. The track they were following was supposed to lead to a ford, but heavy rain had swollen the river to an orange swirling flood when Matt and G-G reached its banks.

"You would need one of my flying ancestors to cross that," G-G said with disappointment. "We will have to search for a better crossing point."

They turned and walked alongside the river looking for a likely place to cross. When they came round a bend a few miles later, they saw a large flat boat on the far bank. There was a thick rope strung across the river, tied to a tree on either bank. A figure was sat hunched in the boat.

"Good day to you sir!" Matt called. "Do you know of any crossing point?"

The figure sat up and sniffed the air. It then jumped up and began pulling on the rope with arms that looked longer and more powerful than any man's that Matt had seen.

"Beware," warned G-G. "That is a Grolk."

"What on earth is a Grolk?"

"It is a tricky beast, mind what you say to it."

The flat boat skimmed across the churning torrent as if it weighed nothing, but, when it came closer, Matt could see that it was quite massive. It must have weighed a great deal and should have been washed away by the surging water, but the rope passed through two sturdy, iron rings that topped posts at either end of the boat. He could also see the

Grolk. It looked something like the apes that Matt had seen in his school books, but it wasn't hairy, its skin was gnarled and scaled like a crocodile's. Its arms were long and muscular. When the Grolk climbed out of its boat and stood up, the knuckles dragged very near to the ground. It was smiling, almost pleasantly, but it was too ugly to ever be really pleasant.

"Good day sir." The Grolk's voice was rough and sounded like pebbles being rolled in a stream. "I can ferry you across and all you will have to pay is with some wise words, if you know any wise words." There was a sort of growling chuckle.

"My good fellow, how kind," Matt still followed his mother's advice. "I am sure we can find something interesting to talk about." The Grolk did not realise that when Matt said 'we' he meant G-G as well. Who knows what he would have done if he knew G-G's true nature.

"Climb aboard then." The Grolk swung onto the ferry, Matt and G-G stepped carefully onto the deck. The muscles on the brawny arms rippled as the Grolk pulled on the rope without much apparent effort. The ferry glided out into the river but, when it was in mid-stream, the Grolk stopped pulling and the ferry stopped.

"Why have we stopped?" Matt asked slightly nervously.

"Now's the time for the wise words," the Grolk said menacingly. "I will only carry you across if you can answer my three riddles."

"And if we cannot answer your riddle?"

"I'll wring your little neck and eat you!" the Grolk snapped and then laughed a horrible, deep throated laugh.

Looking at the powerful arms, Matt gulped. But he had learned to put faith in his ingenuity and tried to control his voice as he said, "OK, and if we do answer the riddle, you promise to carry us to the other side?"

"Of course I will," the Grolk chuckled as if private thoughts amused him.

"Well then, I enjoy playing games even when the stakes seem to be rather high. What is your first riddle?"

"My namesake lives underwater, like a baby he stays on his back kicking his legs. But, if the weather turns warm, like a bird he takes to the air. Who am I?"

Matt scratched his head, the Grolk rubbed his hands together and grinned menacingly, his yellow teeth making a jagged smile. Then Matt smiled an altogether more agreeable smile.

"I spent a lot of my childhood playing by the village pond," he said confidently. "I remember being fascinated by the little creatures that we caught in nets and kept prisoner in jars. One had two long legs that it rowed like oars and, when it came to the surface to breathe, you could see that it was on its back." The Grolk's grin disappeared. "I asked my grandma where they came from and she told me that they were insects and had wings folded inside their case. She said that they could fly from pond to pond, but only in very warm weather. We called it a water boatman, so, the namesake is a boatman, and the answer is you!" Matt pointed triumphantly at the Grolk. The Grolk swore. "Good, I'm right then. Now, what is riddle number two?"

The Grolk swore again. "I've never needed a second riddle," he moaned to himself and slumped down to think. "Ah," he suddenly said as a look of enlightenment spread across his face. "My armoured sides ripple with rain-washed sun. I have no legs or wings, but still chase flies. Men trick me to join them for dinner."

"That's easy," Matt almost jeered, but a look from G-G warned him not to upset the Grolk too much. "I learned to fish with my uncle, he would make imitation flies to catch trout. I was always struck with the beauty of their scales with rainbow markings – it's a rainbow trout."

The Grolk became very unhappy and started beating the floor of the boat. Matt was frightened, but he tried not to show it. The Grolk gave him a long, hard look and his green tongue slid along his thin lips. Matt didn't care to try and read his thoughts. The Grolk sat brooding, then a leer twisted across his face.

"My, we are a clever little person aren't we," the Grolk almost spat the words out. "Try this one: which creature in the morning goes on four feet, at noon on two, and in the evening upon three?" he asked in a voice that seethed with rage.

Matt was stumped, he was expecting another riddle to do with the water. He thought about all the tiny creatures that changed as they grew, from worms to nymphs, to flies. He knew that mayflies only lasted a day, but they had six legs. His face began to look really troubled, the Grolk's face took on a new, eager delight.

"It is you, Matt," G-G spoke suddenly. The Grolk nearly jumped out of the boat. "That is an ancient riddle," G-G explained. "The riddle of the sphinx. At the start of his life, or his day, a man crawls on all fours as a baby. When his sun is at its strongest, he stands erect on two feet. In the evening of his life, he leans upon a stick to help him walk."

"You didn't tell me your horse could speak!" screamed the Grolk. "That's cheating! I'm going to eat both of you!" He raised his arms ready to pounce on Matt who cowered at the bottom of the boat.

"Stay!" commanded G-G. "You know the sacred rules of riddling, a great penalty will befall you if you do not take us across the river." The powerful tone of G-G's voice calmed Matt and he sat up. The Grolk stepped back, a worried look on his face. He spent a few moments thinking over his options and then, reluctantly, he took hold of the rope and began hauling angrily. The ferry shot across the water and collided with the far bank. Matt tumbled over, but G-G stood firm.

"Come Matt," G-G said calmly. "We must be on our way." She stepped majestically over the Grolk who was sat hunched in the prow of the ferry. Matt picked himself up and stumbled as quickly as he could out of the boat.

Just as Matt reached the bank, the Grolk's hand shot out and grabbed his ankle. "I have paid my debt; I have carried you across the river. Now, I'm going to eat you!"

Matt screamed as the bone-crunching grip tightened on his ankle but, suddenly there was a loud sound like a sack of wheat hitting the ground, and the Grolk's hand was no longer there, nor was the Grolk. There was a loud splash as the evil beast hit the water. G-G had kicked him so hard right in the midriff that he had been knocked right out of his boat. The raging river dragged him away, his great arms flailing about trying to swim. Within a few minutes, he was gone. Matt wasn't sure if he would drown, and he didn't really care.

"I owe you my life," said Matt thankfully. "How can I ever repay you?"

"Think nothing of it, that beast should have known that you cannot cheat the sacred rules of riddling. Now, it is time to travel on."

"First I must collect something from this place. I'm not sure why, but it seems that I am destined to go on finding adventures and I always need something that I have brought with me. Matt looked in the bottom of the boat. Apart from a few dirty rags, the only thing there was a strong rope. He picked it up, coiled it and hung it round his shoulder. Then he climbed onto G-G's sturdy back and they set off together.

## Chapter 7 – RETURN

Matt and G-G continued through the forest at a brisker pace, Matt was keen to be home and G-G was happy to oblige. The hills had disappeared behind them and, if Matt was reading the map correctly, they were only a few days from their destination. The rest of the journey passed without incident, just two companions travelling and talking together.

When the track became a lane and he could see wisps of smoke rising above the trees, Matt became excited at the prospect of riding into the village. What a spectacle to impress his neighbours, the traveller returning on a magnificent horse, a talking horse. He imagined all the excited children running up shouting and pointing, asking questions.

When he did finally enter the village, all sorts of people came rushing up, shouting and pointing and asking questions, but they weren't excited, they were angry!

"Why did you do it?"

"What other monsters have you brought with you?"

"What are you going to do about the trouble you've caused?"

Then his mother approached, her face stained with tears. "Oh Matthew, how could you?"

Matt was shocked and bewildered, he even forgot about being called Matt. "How could I do what, mother? Why are all these people so angry?"

"It's that spider," she wailed. "That Gerble or whatever it is called."

"What about Gerble?"

"It's killed one of the children, it's killed Sarah!"

Matt was dumbstruck. He thought that he had defeated Gerble and reduced her to a harmless pet. "But how? Was it a poison bite? What was Sarah doing in my house?"

The mob started shouting again but Matt couldn't make any sense of the confused babble. He held his hands up. "Wait, wait," he shouted. "One at a time, someone please tell me what is going on."

Matt's father was one of the last to arrive. He looked stern and serious. He made his way to the front of the crowd and called for calm. He turned to Matt and spoke in a grim voice. "Oh my son, your foolish adventures have brought great trouble to our village."

"Will someone please tell me what I have done?" Matt pleaded desperately.

His father explained what had happened. Gerble had escaped from Matt's bedroom and fed herself on small creatures that she hunted down. At first it was moths and other insects. As she fed, she had grown, quite quickly. Soon, she was catching mice, then rats. People had thought this was useful and encouraged her to go hunting around the village, but, as she grew, she moved onto larger prey. When she had grown large enough to catch cats and dogs, people had complained and a group of villagers had chased her out of the village. Out in the forest, she had continued to hunt successfully and grown stronger and larger. Gerble had become a real menace. People feared to go into the forest to collect firewood, they could not let their pigs into the forest to forage for acorns. Sheep began disappearing from the pens overnight; Gerble was coming into the village under cover of darkness to feed herself.

"And then," Matt's father continued, shaking his head. "And then, two days ago, Sarah disappeared. She was always a wilful girl and she had boasted to her friends that she was able to talk with the vile creature, stupid girl! Her friends didn't believe her and they teased her, and so she went into the forest to prove them wrong. She has not been seen since." Matt was stunned to see his father's cheeks were wet. The crowd began shouting again.

"Good people." The crowd were stunned into silence when G-G spoke. "Good people, I am sorry to hear of your trouble, but I am sure that Matt will be able to do something, he captured Gerble before."

"And what a sad day that was for our village!" someone shouted. "And now he brings another monster, a talking horse. What do you eat?"

"I can assure you," G-G continued calmly, "I am no threat to any of you."

Matt roused himself out of the shock he had fallen into. "G-G is my friend, he saved my life."

For a moment, the crowd forgot the horror of their situation and several laughed and jeered at the babyish name, but G-G's look and the commanding tone of the way she spoke soon quietened them. "Good people, we have been on a long journey. Let us rest and then we will talk to see how we can defeat this evil monster that Matt has brought into your midst."

There was a great deal of grumbling but, after a few consoling words from his mother, the crowd left Matt and G-G and went back to their houses.

"Oh Matthew," his mother wailed. "Come home and we'll have some tea. What about your horse? We don't have a stable," she flustered.

"It is kind of you to think of my needs," G-G said in a stately voice. "Just water and fresh grass is all I need."

Matt's mother didn't know what to say. She wasn't sure if her rules on how to speak properly to strangers extended to horses, not even talking ones. She scuttled off to put the kettle on. Matt's father put an arm around his son's shoulders and they walked together.

"I don't understand," Matt moaned. "I thought I had defeated Gerble. I wasn't to know that she would do this."

"Perhaps you should have followed your own advice," G-G said firmly. "Never give your enemies a second chance you told Stermian's people. You should have dealt with this spider when you had the opportunity."

"But my mother had always told me that it was unlucky to kill a spider."

"Superstitions, why do you humans allow superstitions to rule your behaviour?" G-G's voice sounded weary.

Matt's mother composed herself by the time she got back to the house and decided that a picnic would allow her to treat her unexpected guest properly. She made some sandwiches quickly, there was always cake in the cupboard, and she had a large bowl that she filled with water.  She was just putting chairs out in the garden when her husband, Matt and G-G arrived.  Matt found the familiarity of the garden very calming, G-G found the grass rather too short and neat to eat easily, but she didn't complain.

Matt and G-G listened patiently while Mr Sadler told them all about what had been happening in the village.  Matt's mother flapped and wailed as Matt told them of his adventures.

"Oh Matthew, why oh why did you have to go to such dangerous places?"

"Oh mother," he began to complain, but a look from G-G stopped him being cross with her.  Instead, he felt guilty about what he had put her and the village through.  "I'm sorry mother," he said softly, and he gave her a hug and dabbed her eyes with his handkerchief.  "Anyway," he stiffened himself.  "I suppose I'd better go and sort out the problem that I have caused."

"Oh no!" moaned his mother.

"Now Mary," said Mr Sadler.  "If Matthew, er, Matt is to be a man, then a man has to do what a man has to do.  He has captured that spider before, on his own.  This time, he will have help, I will go with him, and I presume his noble friend here will also help.  Come on son, it's time to go and sort out this mess."

"Oh, Arthur, you'll all be killed, I just know it!"

"I will make sure they return safely," G-G said in a reassuring voice, but Matt's mother wouldn't be consoled.  As Matt and his father stood up, she grabbed them both and smothered them in a wet hug. They managed to prise themselves away and walked out of the garden. Matt collected the rope that he had hooked onto the garden gate. He wasn't sure what he was going to do, but his instinct told him that he would need the Grolk's rope. He also patted his red bag and the few Granscher scales he had left jingled comfortingly.

As the three of them walked down the street towards the part of the forest where Gerble had last been seen, villagers came out of their houses to watch. Some made angry comments about the curse that Matt had brought to their contented lives. Others clapped encouragement, hoping beyond hope that their nightmare was soon to be over.

## Chapter 8 – CLOSURE

As the three, would be, heroes approached the edge of the forest, their spirits were lifted by the beautiful autumn afternoon. Everything seemed to be normal: a robin was singing sweetly on a high branch, a squirrel scampered round the back of a stout tree as if playing hide and seek. There was no sign of Gerble. As they entered, the floor of the forest was deep in red, yellow and brown leaves that crunched under their feet, but many branches still clung on to their leaves, winter had not quite arrived.

Deeper in the forest, Gerble was aware of their approach as she sat minding her larder in an ancient oak tree, the only one large enough to contain her bloated body. Several silk wrapped cocoons of different shapes and sizes hung from the branches and she caressed one with the tip of a ghastly, hairy leg.

"Ooh yess, here comess ssome more tassty ssnacks to ssee me through the winter. Welcome to my pantry, I may be a sspider, but I eat more than fliess!" she sang quietly to herself.

"Helmm, helmm," muffled cries came from the cocoon and it wriggled like a caterpillar.

"That'ss it, you keep wriggling, then I know you're nicce and fressh. Ooh, look," she crooned. "I know sspiderss are ssuppossed to be lucky, but jusst look, two humanss and a whole juiccy horsse." Gerble shifted her great bulk and tensed herself.

Matt, his father and G-G had relaxed and were walking casually through the forest. There was no sign of any danger ahead of them when Gerble's hindmost legs suddenly jerked into life above them. Two strands of silk, no thicker than spun wool but stronger than steel, were yanked from their hiding place in the crevices of the bark and the trap that lay hidden in the fallen leaves shot upwards.

"Whoa!" Matt's father was scooped up like a tadpole in a child's net. Matt and G-G watched helplessly as he was rolled under Gerble's dreadful abdomen and wrapped quickly in a silk cocoon.

G-G came to her senses and nudged Matt into life. "Quick, we must get clear!"

"Dad!" Matt wailed staring up into the tree.

Gerble stopped immediately. "I know that voicce!" Her own voice seethed with a mixture of venom and fear. "It'ss the one who trapped me before!" She gathered her bundle jealously under her and scuttled higher into the tree.

G-G nudged Matt once more and then pushed him away from the tree. Matt turned, and then ran with G-G trotting beside him. When they reached a clearing, they both stopped and Matt slumped down. There was a long silence with both of them deep in thought. Matt got up suddenly and began pacing back and forth.

"What are we going to do? We must save him." Matt was beside himself.

"We must think clearly," G-G said calmly. "I do not think Gerble will fall into the same mistake as she did the first time you met her. We need some kind of weapon to kill her."

"But my village is a peaceful place," Matt said, almost proudly. "We do not keep weapons."

"How fortunate you are, I wish the rest of the world was such. You have the Granscher scales," G-G was almost thinking out loud.

"I suppose I could use the scales to cut myself a pole and then make a spear by wedging some scales into the end of the pole." Matt thought for a few seconds, but his face fell. "I don't think I'd be any good at throwing a spear, and I certainly wouldn't want to get close enough to that monster to stick it in!"

G-G stood thinking for a while. "You have the Grolk's rope, we could make a ballista."

"A what?"

"A ballista, it is like a large crossbow. My ancestors accompanied armies that used them. All we need are some springy saplings and the rope." G-G scratched a diagram in the brown earth and explained what she intended to do. Matt was not sure, but he trusted his friend.

Gerble sat at the top of her tree, she was worried about the reappearance of her tormentor, but she seethed with thoughts of revenge. The cocoon was still held beneath her vile abdomen, it wriggled and struggled and gave out muffled cries. She looked and listened, there was no sign of Matt and so she clambered back down and hung the cocoon in her larder. Then, very cautiously, she let herself down to the ground, reset her snare and then retreated to the safety of the large boughs of the tree.

Matt and G-G crept back to near where she waited and scouted around for suitable saplings. Gerble was aware of them, but waited, hoping her trap would be sprung again. G-G selected two hazel bushes that had springy poles growing straight up. Then, she raised her head to see over the shrubbery to line up on Gerble's tree, and selected a third bush where the joint of two branches made a crux in the right place. Meanwhile, Matt was busy cutting a straight hazel pole using a Granscher scale. Then he stripped the leaves and twigs from the pole and cut off the whippy topmost part. Lastly, he wedged several scales into the freshly cut tip to make a spear that he held above his shoulder and pretended to throw. His face was set with a grim and determined look.

G-G showed Matt where to tie the rope between the two springy poles and how to load the spear into the ballista so that the whole thing was indeed like a giant crossbow. But, when Matt tried to pull it back he groaned.

"I'll never be strong enough to pull that back and fire the thing!"

"No, but I will," G-G spoke reassuringly. "There is spare rope at the end, cut it off, tie it to the middle of the bow string and then round my neck." G-G stood with her hind quarters close to the ballista rope.

Matt did as he was instructed and then G-G set herself and walked forward impressively. The rope was pulled back and the two springy poles bent. Matt cut a groove in the base end of his spear, set it against the taut rope and rested the lethal tip in the crux of the bush. G-G looked back and shuffled

73

sideways a little to align the spear with Gerble's tree, the top of which she could see above the bushes.

"All we have to do now is be patient. Sooner or later Gerble will come looking for us. When she does, you cut the rope around my neck and the ballista will fire." G-G sounded so confident, but Matt's face showed doubt. "Be positive, think back on all the tales you have told me. You have succeeded in every trial so far."

Matt felt slightly more at ease and settled down to wait. G-G relaxed backwards to relieve the tension on the rope.

All this time, Gerble was sat in her tree, idly poking the wriggling cocoons. She was brooding on the time she had spent imprisoned in Matt's cup and dreaming of tormenting him, wrapped up tight with her other meals, such a sweet dream to such a disgusting creature. She savoured the thought so much and found it so enjoyable just to dream about it, she was prepared to be patient.

Matt began to fidget; he was worried about his father. Would he be in time to save him? Was he suffering? Matt jumped up and paced around.

"I think we need to bait this trap," he said sternly. Then he marched halfway towards the tree but still with a bush shielding him from Gerble's direct sight. He sat down on a log and began to whistle, rather weakly at first, but then more loudly.

Gerble stopped toying with the cocoons and hissed. What was going on? Why was the human whistling? She peered around, but could see nothing. Finally, her curiosity got the better of her and she scuttled down the tree, the jagged tips of her legs gripping the cracks of the bark. At the foot of the tree, she stopped and looked around warily, but she still couldn't see anything. Matt's whistling was coming from behind a nearby bush. Gerble's fangs began to dribble and she crept forward.

The faint rustle of her claws in the leaves on the forest floor alerted G-G. Once more, she tensed and walked forward to set the ballista, taking care to stand in the same spot as before to keep the aim true. Matt heard the creak of the bending poles behind him and looked back. When he turned round again, he fell back with a scream; Gerble had raised herself to her full monstrous height and towered over the bush in front of Matt's sprawling body. She hissed with delight, but Matt scrambled backwards and managed to get to his feet. He ran to stand beside G-G and was about to cut the retraining rope when G-G stopped him.

"Wait! She's too high!" It was the first time that Matt had heard anything approaching concern or worry in G-G's voice.

Gerble hissed and dribbled and her eyes sparkled with joy. She bent her long hairy legs and lowered her massive body, crushing the bush. She stalked forward, relishing the thought of sucking the juice from this troublesome little creature. The horse would be a bonus.

"Now!" G-G shouted. Matt's hand swooped down and the Granscher scale in his hand sliced through the rope like a knife through butter. There was a twang and G-G lurched forward as the tension was released.  The spear shot forward and disappeared completely into Gerble's face.  She let out a blood curdling scream, shuddered and staggered forward.  Matt stood, frozen to the spot as she continued to lurch forward.  Then she stumbled on the ballista rope and fell forward with a sickening crunching sound and crashed to the ground with her terrible fangs either side of Matt's feet.  Just as the first time he had met her, Matt just stood petrified in front of Gerble.  He was staring down into those five malicious eyes, but this time they dulled one by one.

G-G recovered herself and rushed to Matt's side, ready to use her hooves to defend him, but Gerble lay completely still.

"She's dead!" G-G nudged Matt who snapped out of his terror and jumped back.  An evil smelling black liquid was oozing from the wound where the spear had entered and it was dribbling and soaking into the soft brown earth of the forest floor.  A soft moaning, wailing whisper seemed to come from underground.  At the same time, Gerble's body began to shrink like some grotesque balloon deflating, but the body was reducing far more than could be accounted for by the loss of the black liquid.  Soon, the ends of the spear were protruding from the remains, but the body continued to shrink.  Then the skin was tight around the shaft of the spear and, finally, it split and shrivelled to leave the tattered remnants of an ordinarily sized spider beside the now blackened spear.

"There was a great evil here," G-G intoned seriously.  "There was a malevolent spirit inside that spider. Something that strengthened it and made it more than it would have been."

Matt sat down wearily. "The only thing that I care about is that Gerble is definitely dead!"

"She may be, I only hope the driving spirit is dead too." G-G sounded unsure.

Then Matt jumped to his feet once more. "Dad!" He rushed to the tree and looked up. The sight of all the cocoons hanging there made him feel sick. "Dad!" he shouted once more. The largest of the cocoons wriggled. Matt clambered up the tree, wedging his hands and feet into the same deep crevices that had enabled Gerble's agile descent. He nearly fell as he reached across to the cocoon and pulled it towards him. Muffled cries came from inside. Matt was about to cut the thread that suspended his father when G-G once more stopped his impetuous action.

"The fall will kill him!"

Matt hesitated, confused as to what to do. He was desperate to free his father from the terrible fate that his own stupidity had brought about.

"Cut open the cocoon," G-G was calm once again. "But be careful."

Matt reached into the red bag that was still slung around his shoulder and found his last Granscher scale. As carefully as he could, he sliced into the cocoon, but his hands were trembling.

"Ouch!" His father called out and a small red stain spread on the edges of the cut threads. Matt pulled the threads apart and his father's head struggled out of the hole. He had a small cut on his cheek and he was gasping for breath. Matt held back, not wanting to injure his father any more. "Well, get on with it, don't worry about a small scratch," his father said impatiently. "Get me out of here!"

Matt continued cutting and, soon, he and his father were hugging each other as they stood on the broad bough of the tree. Then another cocoon wriggled. This one was out of reach and so, while his father climbed gingerly down from the tree, Matt crawled over several branches to get to the cocoon. By the time he reached it, the wriggling had stopped. He pulled it towards him and, his hands now much steadier, he cut very carefully. He nearly fell out of the tree when Sarah's gaunt face appeared at the hole. She was a grey colour and her eyes were closed. Matt slashed desperately at the cocoon and managed to half catch the limp body as it tumbled out. He fell back and there was an oof as Sarah landed on her stomach across the branch. She began gasping and groaning and her face changed from grey to a pale green, and then a flushed pink, but she was still unconscious. He wasn't sure why, but Matt began to cry.

It wasn't easy, but Matt used the rope and lowered Sarah's limp body to the ground. His father tended to her while Matt checked the other cocoons. It was nearly dark by the time he had managed to check them all. They contained a variety of animals. Sadly, many were dead, but a badger, a piglet and a fawn were still kicking. Matt lowered them to the ground, his father pulled the threads apart and the animals struggled free, rushing off into the forest.

Sarah had come round while he was doing that. When Matt noticed her, she was sat up just watching him. With his help, she was strong enough to sit on G-G's back and they all set off back to village.

## Chapter 9 – REST

Many of the villagers had stayed gossiping on the street or in their gardens the whole afternoon and into the evening. Groups came together and moved apart, most of the conversation was gloomy.

"I always said that Matthew Sadler would come to a bad end," said Tomasina the butcher's wife.

"That's funny," sneered her husband. "I thought you told me I ought to go and find some gold." His wife swung a meaty arm and thumped his shoulder.

"I don't know," Will the farrier shook his head, "All youngsters these days have lost respect for their elders, *I* wouldn't have gone off when *I* was younger."

"Well the second part's certainly true," Tomasina scoffed.

"Oh these are terrible days," Susie the dressmaker shook her head. "Giant spiders, talking horses, whatever next?"

Matt's mother hid in her neat little house, she could not talk to anyone, she wept with a mixture of shame and fear. She had launched into a fit of distracted cleaning. Every piece of crockery had been washed and dried and every stick of furniture had been moved and dusted behind. The linen cupboard had been emptied of its neat piles of bedding and the whole lot had been pressed again and returned in even neater piles. But, if you had asked her, Matt's mother could not have told you what she had just been doing, her mind was lost in the forest.

"Mary! Mary, come quick, they're back!" A neighbour had rushed into the kitchen. Matt's mother dropped the cup that was being dried for the third time, and she stood there, not able to move or understand. The neighbour grabbed her arm and literally dragged her out of the door.

"Oh my good Lord!" Matt's mother gasped. An excited crowd was gathered at the far end of the village, and in the middle she could see G-G with a girl on her back, and, yes, it was Sarah! "Oh thank you, thank you, thank you!" she sobbed as she looked up to the sky. She rubbed her hands on her apron as she began to run. She ran as she had not run for twenty years. She pushed her way through the crowd, forgetting all that she had ever said about politeness and what she called decorum. She flung her arms out and grabbed her Matthew and, sobbing tears of relief, she smothered him with kisses.

Had it been the previous day, Matt would have pushed her out at arm's length, today he just surrendered to his own emotions and his eyes filled.

There was a scream along the street and everyone turned to see Sarah's mother rushing wildly towards them. G-G bent her front legs and Sarah slid carefully down, helped by one of the villagers. When she embraced her mother, a burst of spontaneous clapping and cheering spread through the crowd.

Sarah's mother turned to Matt. "Oh, Matthew Sadler, however can I thank you for rescuing my dear, lovely Sarah?" She gave him a tight hug that Matt just accepted without protest.

"It was the least I could do," said Matt humbly. "I brought that awful monster into your lives, and so I had the responsibility for getting rid of it."

Sarah, still weak from her ordeal, leaned against Matt. "Oh, you're such a brave hero, Matthew." She had a dreamy, far away look in her eyes, which Matt put down to the shock of being smothered in that awful cocoon.

"Would you like a cup of tea, Arthur, love?" This was the first time that anyone had actually acknowledged Matt's father, but he didn't mind, he was just proud of his son.

"That would be lovely, Mary. Come on everyone, it's all over now, and it's late, you should be putting your children to bed."

There was a babble of questions and comments as the rescue party and the crowd made their way towards the Sadler's cottage.

"I always said that Mr and Mrs Sadler had done a brilliant job in bringing up their son," said Will the farrier. "Our village has the bravest and kindest, most caring children in all the world."

"My distant relatives will be so jealous," chuckled Susie the dressmaker. "I can't wait to write and tell them about our very own talking horse." Tomasina gave them both a sideways look and she tutted.

The crowd began drifting away, talking excitedly in small groups as the Sadler family, Sarah's family and G-G went through the gate. The two families sat in the garden with G-G and talked together late into the night. When Matt's mother brought out blankets to keep themselves warm, Sarah and Mr

Sadler were not very keen on being wrapped up again. Instead, Matt used his new-found skills and built a small fire. No-one minded that it scorched a patch of the neatly tended lawn, they were just happy to be together.

Over the coming days, things gradually settled down and the village went back to its sleepy, unexciting normality. Matt stayed at his parents' house. He was embarrassed when he went out because people would nudge each other knowingly if they saw him walking along the street. Children hung on the gate and leaned over the garden fence, asking if he would tell them about the giant spider. Matt shooed them away. Sarah would walk by regularly and she would gather the children together, sit them down and tell them all about how wonderful Matt had been.

"But you were wrapped in the cocoon, how could you know what was happening?" one child had asked after hearing the story for a fifth time.

"You can see and hear through spider's web, you silly little boy!" she had dismissed him crossly and he went bight red. "If you ever find yourself in situation like that, you'll know if someone brave and handsome is coming to your rescue, you'll just know." The dreamy look was back in her eye. The children giggled.

One of the local farmers gave G-G a large field of the finest pasture. Several villagers worked together and built her a solid and comfortable stable. The children of the village would come by on their way to and from school and she would allow them to climb on her back from the fence that was there to keep other animals out rather than keep G-G in.

When it was quiet, with all the children in school, Matt would wander down to see her. He would sit on the fence and they would have private conversations such as can only be had by characters who had been through so much together.

Mr and Mrs Sadler would watch their son and smile at each other.

"You know Mary, our Matt has grown into a fine young man."

"Yes Arthur," and she gave her husband a quick hug, something she had fallen out of the habit of doing for quite a long time before that day.

Autumn passed into winter. Life went on in the village and all the conversations turned towards the mid-winter festival.

Although he still had enough gold to be comfortable, Matt decided that he needed a trade to occupy him, and so he joined the village carpenter as an apprentice. One of the first things he had to learn was how to sharpen his tools. The one remaining Granscher scale that Matt still possessed never seemed to need sharpening, but chisels and plane blades were a different matter.

The following spring, anemones and bluebells carpeted the forest floor – except for one patch near an old oak tree. Nothing grew there and the animals would not go near it.

Sometimes, but not very often, adventurous children would go and play in the forest. They would climb the old oak tree to swing on the strange stretchy ropes that straggled from some of its larger branches.

If they sat and rested leaning against the great trunk, some children claimed to be able to hear a whispering sound. The sensible ones said it was just the breeze blowing through the leaves…

THE AUTHOR.

Ed Dolphin grew up in Southend-on-Sea in Essex at a time when children played outside more than they do now. He would spend hours each weekend between the sea and the woods finding out about the animals and plants that shared his world and building dens to live out imaginary adventures.

If the tide was out, and it goes out a long way at Southend, he would ride his bike down to the beach and walk out on the sand and mud flats looking for lugworms and shrimps. His strongest memories are of blistering sunburn one Sunday when he'd been out for twelve hours, and finding a bomb sticking out of the sand off the army ranges at Shoebury.

If the tide was in, he wasn't interested in making sand castles. Instead, he would walk to the top of his road and he would be in farmland. The ancient track of Rebels' Lane took him to a small wood scattered with logs to be turned over to reveal woodlice, millipedes and centipedes, and three water filled bomb craters that swarmed with newts and toads each spring. Sadly, too many newts ended their days mummified under kitchen furniture after they had escaped from the small aquarium that was on the worktop.

Ed's love of nature was extended into studying zoology and botany at university, but he dropped out to become a seafront bingo caller. This gave him the chance to study the most fascinating seaside life form, day trippers. When he finally grew up, if he ever really did, Ed decided that there was more to life than bingo calling and he spent over thirty years teaching in Essex and Derbyshire. He took early retirement in 2007, but still keeps in touch with the world of education as a governor of his local school and a part-time tutor on the Graduate Teacher Programme at Derby University.

Ed's first published book, Sophie's Badgers, came out of those early excursions into the local woods. Matt Sadler owes more to Ed's love of old stories and his reservations about celebrity culture.